The Friendly Creeper Diaries,

Book 1: The Creeper Village

Mark Mulle

PUBLISHED BY:

Mark Mulle

Copyright © 2016

To get a FREE book and be updated on Mark Mulle's books
and latest releases, check markmulle.com

TABLE OF CONTENTS

Book 1: The Creeper Village

Day 1

Tomorrow will be the start of a new journey. I don't know what we will discover as we leave our Creeper village in search of answers regarding the recent attacks. I only hope that we, who volunteered to do this, will come home safe and sound.

Day 7

I'm writing this by the campfire. It's growing dark and I have tried to make a shelter but I'm not very good at it. That was always Beth's job. But since we've all gotten separated, I don't know where anyone is.

Okay. Maybe I should start at the beginning. I'm trying not to be nervous about the fact that I'm in a jungle, but it's hard! At least I have this journal, right? It'll be a distraction, at least.

We set out about a week ago. Leaving the village was a big deal. We had never left before. No, we had always stuck to ourselves. It was because we aren't like most of the other creepers—we're friendly. But no one tends to actually believe that we aren't going to blow up around things because of their experiences with all the other creepers. So we went off and formed our own village up in the mountains. It was away from everyone else and we were safe.

Up until recently. Lately, our village has

been under attack by creatures from the Nether. I don't know how that could be. No one does, really. We had never had creatures from the Nether in the Over World and for them to attack us, out of all the places, was so strange.

So, the entire village fought. No one knew what else to do. Our supplies were almost out because we'd been going through so much due to the attacks. We couldn't locate where the enemies were coming from. Some people wanted to go to the Nether but that was quickly shot down.

Finally, we decided that a group would go down the mountain and to the nearest village to see if they were having any problems like we were. They were taking sign-ups. I wasn't ready to go. Going out of the village and into the unknown? Where everyone thought we were creatures that just exploded? No, thank you.

I was walking past the village square when I heard someone call my name.

"Mike!"

I turned around and saw my friend, Alex, coming over to me. I had known him since we were kids and already knew what he was going to tell me before he even opened his mouth.

"You signed up yet?" he asked.

"No. I'm not going to sign up."

"What? You have to! We can finally see the rest of the Over World this way!"

"Yeah and loads of other things that want to attack us," I pointed out. "You want me down there with people who think we just explode on sight or Nether creatures chasing after us? What if we get down there and the Nether is all over the place?"

"Well, then we know we aren't alone. And we can try to help out. I'm going to sign up now. Come on."

He grabbed my arm and tugged me along the small village square. The rest of the creepers were talking in low voices and in small groups. No one had volunteered yet. Everyone was nervous about the idea of leaving the village.

Alex yanked me to the piece of paper stuck to the stone wall of the mayor's house and glanced at me.

"I'm signing up," he announced loudly, causing some of the other creepers to look over.

I was about to tell him to forget it, no way was I going to sign up with him, when the mayor's door opened and out came Beth. Beth looked over at the two of us.

"You two volunteering?" she asked.

"Yes, ma'am. Mayor." Alex said quickly.

"That's great," Beth replied and walked over to the paper, "I am as well. I am the mayor, after all."

This caused the other creepers nearby to start speaking in louder voices. No one had expected our own mayor to sign up! She scribbled down her name and so did Alex. He thrust the pen towards me.

How could I back out now? The mayor had signed up along with us. It would look terrible to suddenly back out. Maybe Alex was right—it would be dangerous but we would see all sorts of new and fantastic things out there.

So I wrote my name down.

Instantly, there was a hum of activity. Eight more creepers came over and wrote their name down as well. All the slots filled up within minutes. It was official. I was going out to see the rest of the Over World.

A few days later, we were all set to head

out. We had to scale down the mountain first, which was secretly terrifying me. Because we had a full amount of creepers sign up, one group was going to head towards the villages by the sea and we were going to head towards the one in the jungle.

The mountain was steep but there was an old pathway that we took. Beth led our group. At least we had the mayor with us. Alex was thrilled to be out of the village and heading down the mountain. I still couldn't believe I had somehow gotten sucked into this.

"Do you think we're going to figure out

why creatures from the Nether are attacking us?" Alex asked as we worked our way down the mountain.

"I don't know," I replied. "Maybe. I get that we have to go see if anyone can help us but I'm still nervous."

"Because we're creepers?"

"Well, yeah. I mean, as far as we know, everyone down there thinks we're hostile. They think we're going to blow up as soon as they see us."

"Right, so we'll just have to change their minds."

"I guess so."

We walked in silence for a bit as the mountain sloped downwards. Ahead of us were Beth, Adam, Derek, and Sue. Beth was leading the way and the rest of us trailed behind her. I wondered if anyone else was nervous about the fact we were going into a jungle.

"Aren't jungles filled with spiders and skeletons?" I wondered aloud.

"Yeah, but we can take them," Alex boasted.

In front of us, Sue glanced back at us,

"We aren't going to fight. We'll make sure we have shelter each night and are safe and sound."

That was a relief, at least. Night did come and like Sue had said we had a shelter up and were safely inside before anything could come out of the darkness. As we snuggled down into bed, a thought struck me.

"Do you think Nether creatures will be walking around the mountain?"

"Mike, don't," Derek spoke up, "or I'll never be able to sleep."

That made two of us.

Day 8

I got too tired to finish last night. I ended up falling asleep by the campfire. This morning I managed to find some food to eat then I set out across the stream to see if I could find anyone from our group. No such luck. I'm starting to panic now. Derek had the map and all the location information of where we were heading.

Okay. Writing in this helps me a bit so I will keep going with what happened.

We woke up that morning on the mountain and the sun was high in the sky. We had made it through the night! No Nether creatures or anything. Maybe it really is just our village after all.

We made our way down the mountain that day and entered the jungle that night. We quickly put up a shelter and spent the night. The next day, we took off to enter the jungle.

The jungle was completely different than the mountain or our little village. The air was humid and heavy. It felt as if we had stepped into a world covered with a giant blanket. The trees were so tall and sometimes the sun could barely get through to light the way. There were a lot of different noises too.

"I think we go this way," Beth said halfway through the day, pointing to the right.

"You think?" Adam asked, sounding nervous.

"Yeah, I mean…" She twisted the map around a few times, as if trying to make sense of it—which, let me tell you, wasn't very comforting.

"No, you're reading that wrong," Sue said and took the map from Beth.

"How?"

"Look, we're here, not here."

The two of them bent their heads over the map, looking at it. I glanced over at Alex. For once, he did look a little worried.

"Guys, it's going to get dark if we don't at least make camp," I finally spoke up.

"Mike is right," Alex agreed.

"Yeah, guys, we should go right," Beth said.

"That's the wrong way."

"Guys—"

That was when we heard the boom. It was so loud that Alex ducked, as if something was being thrown at us. Something about the noise sounded oddly familiar, although I couldn't place why. Everyone looked around, silent and startled.

Then we heard it. It sounded like bones moving together. It sounded like a skeleton.

"But it's daytime!" Sue exclaimed, shocked.

That was the last thing I heard before the

chaos took over. The first wither skeleton came through from the left. It was tall and holding a sword. Our group turned to the right to flee but another wither skeleton had appeared there as well.

"This is not good," I mumbled to Alex.

"You think?" he remarked.

"This way!" Beth said and took off into the jungle.

However, she was running towards where the booming noise had come from. Somehow, I thought that taking off towards the noise that sent the wither skeletons to us was a bad idea. Apparently Alex thought so too because he grabbed my arm and we took off running through the jungle.

The wither skeleton on the left swung at us. We ducked but we both lost our footing. We weren't exactly used to dodging wither skeletons in the jungle. Suddenly, I was toppling down a hill. Alex was rolling along next to me. I tried to grab onto something but no luck.

With a painful thud, we both landed at the base of the hill. We were in a stream. I managed to scramble to my feet and help Alex up.

"You okay?" I asked.

"I think so. You?"

"Yeah, just sore." I looked up at the top of the hill. "Uh, we have bigger issues though."

The wither skeleton was running down the hill towards us. It is faster than us and skilled at moving around the terrible jungle floor. Before Alex could say anything in reply, I started tugging him forward.

We ran through the jungle blindly, trying to shake off the wither skeleton, which seemed determined to track us down. We crashed through some thick leaves and stumbled into a clearing.

There was a shift in the trees and a rustling noise. Then something came out of the leaves. Alex let out a startled noise. At first I thought that he was part of our group but then I realized he looked different than we did. It was a creeper. A creeper! Someone not from our village. Just a wild creeper that lived out here in the jungle. He was staring at us. Was he confused? Did he wonder why we were here?

I opened my mouth to speak but that was when the wither skeleton crashed through and entered the clearing. Alex yanked me back as the wither skeleton came toward us. Then it saw the other creeper. This creeper was heading toward the three of us now. His eyes were red and he didn't say anything.

The wither skeleton swung its sword but by then it was too late. The creeper was making a strange noise that I realized meant it was going to explode.

"Run!" I shouted at Alex and pushed him out of the way.

Alex crashed through the leaves. The creeper behind me suddenly exploded and I was sent flying through the air. I couldn't see anything. It was all a big green blur.

Then I crashed to the ground. I got a mouthful of dirt which I spit up right away and looked around. I didn't see anyone. Didn't even hear anything. No creeper. No wither skeleton. I wanted to start shouting people's names but what if there were other Nether creatures there waiting to hear something? Or another creeper, which apparently didn't care if we were also creepers—he was going to blow up anyway.

I sat up and looked around. The trees

here were so thick that it was almost pitch dark. I got to my feet and walked around a little bit. I was really sore but was okay. Creeper skin is extra thick so even if we explode around each other, we aren't hurt like humans are. Never thought I'd have to experience that first hand, though.

That was when I managed to find a little overhang for a shelter. The rock jutted out and made it easy to sort of make a wall out of rocks and branches. Once I realized no one was coming after me and it was growing dark quickly, I made a campfire.

This is where I have been the past two days. I kept waiting around hoping that someone was going to show up but it's starting to look like I'm going to have to take off into the jungle and try to find the group.

Day 9

In the morning, I set out to try to find everyone. Maybe the explosion had sent me far off track and that was why no one had stumbled across me yet? Or was that just wishful thinking? In any case, two days of sitting around a campfire was long enough. I needed to make things happen.

The hard thing about making things

happen while being stuck in a jungle is that I wasn't even sure where to set off to make things happen. I could go back the way I thought the explosion had sent me flying and try to backtrack from there. Alex could still be around there, hopefully.

I decided that would be the best bet. If there were more wither skeletons floating around, I would have to try to avoid them seeing me. Why were they in the jungle? Why were they coming after us? More questions were forming being away from the village instead of being answered.

It took a little bit to get back to the clearing. Apparently that creeper blast had sent me flying. When I finally got to the clearing it was empty. There was some kicked up dirt from where the creeper had exploded but nothing else. No wither skeleton. No Alex.

"Alex?" I hissed, trying to keep my voice low. "you here?"

No answer. I didn't really expect Alex to be there after two days. He probably had tried to find me as well. We must have each gone in different directions. I went off in the direction that I had shoved him when the creeper was about to explode.

It was another hill. I made sure to walk down this one slowly. I really didn't want to topple down yet another hill in the jungle. At the bottom of the hill, things looked more of the same. I was starting to worry now. How was I going to find anyone in this thick jungle? I crossed across another stream and came to a sudden stop.

In front of me was what looked like a giant old building. No, the closer I looked at it, the more I realized that it looked more like a temple. I had read about temples in the jungle but had never thought I'd see one! Excited, I walked towards the entrance. Surely my friends would have formed a base here. It would offer shelter.

As I stepped towards the entrance, there was a strange noise. It sounded like some sort of animal. Instantly, I began to back away from the temple. Then there was the noise of what sounded like metal on stone and suddenly someone burst out of the entrance.

It was a boy, around my age. He was dirty and wearing torn armor. He was clutching a sword. Behind him was a wither skeleton, chasing him down. The boy's eyes widened at the sight of me. I realized he probably thought I was going to explode or something.

I didn't waste any time. I turned around and began to run as well. The wither skeleton was hot on our heels as the boy and I crashed through the jungle. I heard a thud behind me and saw that the boy had fallen.

The wither skeleton had been slowed down a bit by how thick the foliage was. I turned around and grabbed the boy. He let out a yelp of surprise and closed his eyes, as if he was expecting he blast.

"Get up!" I shouted.

His eyes went so wide that I thought they were going to pop out of his head. He got up with my help and we took off running again. The wither skeleton was having a hard time following us. The area the boy was taking us through was filled with streams and vines that made movement slow. I looked back and saw that the wither skeleton had gotten tangled up in some vines and was having a hard time getting out.

"This way!" the boy shouted at me, pointing to the right.

"Up the hill?" I asked, eying it warily.

The wither skeleton was starting to swing its sword to get out of the vines. No time to waste. I nodded and took off running again with the boy. The hill was steep. The boy seemed to be able to climb it easily. He used some of the vines to help him propel forward.

However, I wasn't as skilled at climbing around the jungle as the boy was. The wither skeleton had broken free of the vines and was running towards us again. I was scrambling to get up the hill when I lost my footing. I could feel the dirt move underneath my feet and I was starting to fall backward when the boy reached out and grabbed my arm.

He yanked me forward and I managed to scuttle up to the top of the hill just as the wither skeleton was swinging his sword. It went into the ground and got stuck in the dirt. As the skeleton struggled to get his sword out of the dirt, the boy kicked it. The skeleton was surprised and went flying down the hill.

We were off running again. We ducked and dodged the tree branches and the vines. I glanced behind me and didn't see any sign of the wither skeleton. Maybe we had finally lost him.

"Just ahead!" the boy shouted back at me.

I nodded. I was so out of breath that it felt like I wouldn't be able to talk again. After a couple more minutes of running, we slowed to a jog. Then we broke through the end of the jungle.

The view took my breath away. We were up high on a hill. Down below was a small village. Behind the village was more jungle but there were tall, thick walls surrounding the village. There was a lake near it as well, which was glittering in the sunlight like a jewel. I just stared at it, lost for words. I had never seen anything like this before!

The boy stuck out his hand to me. "David."

I looked down at his hand. I realized he wanted me to shake it or something. I took his hand and sort of shook it which made him frown before he started to laugh.

"I'm Mike," I replied.

"A creeper that can talk?" He shook his head. "Never heard of such a thing. I thought for sure when I saw you that I was done for!"

"You haven't seen any other creepers, have you?" I asked, thinking about Alex and the others.

David looked thoughtful for a moment. "I ran into one a couple days ago. He almost got me too. He exploded just as I climbed up a tree."

"No," I sighed, "we don't explode."

"At all?"

"That's right."

"How come I've never heard of creepers that can talk and don't explode?" David asked.

"We live up on the mountain, away from everyone. But we've run into trouble recently."

"Come on, let's go back to the village and we can talk along the way."

We headed towards a pathway that wound its way down the hill towards the village. I glanced behind me at the jungle but there were no signs of the wither skeleton. I looked back at David.

"Hey, are there normally wither skeletons in there?" I asked.

"No! They've been coming out of the jungle recently. I was trying to figure out why. I thought maybe they had something to do with the temple in there but I didn't see anything connecting to the Nether. And that wither skeleton came out of nowhere."

I told him about why we were in the jungle and how we were spilt up. As we walked, David looked as if he was listening intently. It was strange to be talking to a human like this. I had thought for sure he would have run off screaming but he seemed to be listening to me about everything going on.

Finally, I finished my story.

David spoke. "You know, that sounds

exactly like what's going on here. We've been having Nether creatures come out of the jungle and head into the village. We weren't sure why."

"So they sent you off into the jungle to try to find out?"

"Well," at this David looked sheepish. "I snuck out. My aunt is totally going to freak on me when we get back home. There is no way she's going to be happy with me for sneaking out into the jungle but I felt like I had a good idea everyone was ignoring. Would have been better if I had found out something."

"You found me," I said, trying to be helpful. "Maybe if they see me and hear what I told you, that might help."

"Yeah, maybe," David said, nodding.

The walk to the village was uneventful. Even though I was glad to be out of the jungle, I was worried about not having found anyone from my group yet.

"Do you think someone from my group could have ended up at your village?" I asked David.

"Maybe. If the wither skeletons chased them out, they could have ended back down at the village."

"I guess we'll find out," I replied, trying to sound hopeful.

When the village was closer, I could make things out a bit clearer. The walls around the village looked new. David seemed to sense what I was thinking and he told me they had been reinforced to be stronger once the Nether creatures had begun attacking.

Then I saw a group of people along the top of the wall. They were shouting at someone near the entrance. I frowned and then began to jog forward. David took off after me.

"Alex?" I yelled.

Alex turned around and looked relieved to see me. David was shouting at the people at the top of the wall, trying to explain we weren't regular creepers. Everyone looked confused as they stared at us.

"I've been trying to get out of the jungle since we got spilt up," Alex said to me. "Is anyone else with you?"

"No. I ran into David and was heading here to try to see if any of you guys were here too. The jungle isn't safe. It's full of wither skeletons."

"I know. I barely got out of there safely. When I saw the village, I had to come down here and see if anyone else was here."

"At least we found each other," I said, happy that I found Alex.

There was a loud noise from the village wall. The doors slowly opened. David motioned for the two of us to come over.

"Stay by my side, okay? No one is exactly sure what to make of two creepers who can talk and aren't going to explode."

We nodded and kept close to David as we stepped inside the village. This village looked different from ours. Their building materials were better than what we have and some of their houses were two stories! They even had stores in the center of town.

Everyone in the village seemed to stop and stare at us. Some people looked scared. Others just curious. I could hear some people mumbling.

"David is back."

"Margery is going to be furious with him for sneaking out."

"Are those really creepers?"

We ended up in the center of the village.

There was one house there that was larger than the rest. It looked very official and I wondered if it was where the mayor was. That was when the doors burst open and an old woman came out onto the steps. She had a badge on her chest that made it clear that she was the mayor.

She stared at David, looking furious. "Get in here, boy!"

David looked over at us sheepishly,."My aunt."

"Your aunt is the mayor?" I whispered.

We trudged off towards the house.

Day 10

We all sat down at the table in the kitchen. Margery was getting out food—a lot of it. At the sight of it, my stomach grumbled. She put down fresh milk, vegetables, and pork chops. Then she looked at Alex and I.

"Come on, dig in."

Alex glanced at me, clearly surprised she didn't seem too bothered by two creepers about to eat some food in her kitchen. David was digging in. She sat down and drummed her fingers along the table.

"David, how many times did I tell you not to go off into the jungle?"

"I know," he replied, "but I wanted to look at the jungle temple and no one else wanted to –"

"You're too young to be going off into the jungle by yourself."

"I know but look, I found Mike! He said his village has been having the same issues as us."

Margery looked at me now. "Is this true?"

"Yes, ma'am. We live up on the mountains and came down here for help. Our group got spilt up in the jungle."

Behind me, Alex was nodding. She looked at the two of us and leaned back in her chair. I was too hungry to put it off any longer and began to eat some of the bread and cheese she had put out.

"I'm afraid we don't have any answers either, although knowing it's happening somewhere else is worrisome," she said.

David spoke up, his mouth full of pork chop. "Wither skeletons are only in the Nether. So it has to be connected to them coming into the Over World."

"Right before we were attacked the first time, there was this large booming noise in the jungle. Then the skeletons appeared," I told them.

"That's right," Alex said. "And that's when we got spilt up."

"The village is on edge, of course, seeing as you two are creepers. But you're safe here. I can get a group together and we can try to find the rest of your team in the jungle."

"I want to go—"

"No, David. You're grounded. And I don't want to hear about it any longer. Now, I'll get your rooms together for you to get some rest."

Margery stood up and went down the hallway. I watched her go and then looked back at David. He didn't look that bothered about being grounded.

He caught me staring at him and shrugged a little. "I get grounded a lot."

After we ate, we were shown to our

rooms. Alex and I were sharing a room. He leapt into bed and snuggled up under the sheets. I looked around the room. There was a bookshelf against one side piled up with books. Some of them looked ancient. The other side of the room had a small desk with fresh flowers on it. It was cozy and unlike the rooms back in our village.

"I'm exhausted," Alex remarked.

"Me too," I admitted.

"I know it's early but I'm going to bed," he said with a yawn.

That actually sounded like a good idea. I

could do with some sleep that wasn't on the jungle floor or being panicked about wither skeletons surprising me in the night. I let out a yawn and then I curled up in bed. Before I knew it, I was fast asleep. I didn't dream or wake up once. I slept solidly through the night. When my eyes finally opened, sunlight was pouring through the window. I sat up and looked around. Alex was gone. I assumed that he went back to stuff his face again. He always had a healthy appetite.

I looked out the window. The window looked out over some fields. People were farming in them, pulling up roots or picking fruit. My stomach grumbled. Even though I had stuffed my face last evening, I was already hungry again. There hadn't been much to eat in the jungle.

I turned around and that was when I heard the noise. A giant booming noise seemed to shake the house. I almost fell over from the noise. I ran out to the dining room and that was when Alex and David burst in through the back door. David was pale and Alex looked scared.

"What's going on?" I asked.

"A Nether portal opened up in the

middle of town!" Alex exclaimed.

Mike and his friend, Alex, have found safety in a human village with their new human friend, David. However, just as soon as they get settled, the village is under attack by the Nether! They quickly learn that the wither skeletons are coming after them only. Why are the wither skeletons after Mike and Alex?

READ ALL ABOUT IT in

THE FRIENDLY CREEPER DIARIES, BOOK 2: THE WITHER SKELETON ATTACK

Made in the USA
San Bernardino, CA
13 December 2019